Katie Kazoo,
SWITCHEROO

Vote for ~~Katie~~ Suzanne

GROSSET & DUNLAP

Published by the Penguin Group

Penguin Group (USA) Inc., 375 Hudson Street, New York, New York 10014, USA

Penguin Group (Canada), 90 Eglinton Avenue East, Suite 700, Toronto,
Ontario M4P 2Y3, Canada
(a division of Pearson Penguin Canada Inc.)

Penguin Books Ltd., 80 Strand, London WC2R 0RL, England

Penguin Group Ireland, 25 St. Stephen's Green, Dublin 2, Ireland
(a division of Penguin Books Ltd.)

Penguin Group (Australia), 250 Camberwell Road, Camberwell,
Victoria 3124, Australia
(a division of Pearson Australia Group Pty. Ltd.)

Penguin Books India Pvt. Ltd., 11 Community Centre, Panchsheel Park,
New Delhi—110 017, India

Penguin Group (NZ), 67 Apollo Drive, Rosedale, North Shore 0632, New Zealand
(a division of Pearson New Zealand Ltd.)

Penguin Books (South Africa) (Pty.) Ltd., 24 Sturdee Avenue,
Rosebank, Johannesburg 2196, South Africa

Penguin Books Ltd., Registered Offices: 80 Strand, London WC2R 0RL, England

Library of Congress Control Number: 2007046912

ISBN 978-0-448-44678-3   10 9 8 7 6 5 4

For Ian and his pals in the RSS class of 2008.
Congrats, everyone!—N. K.

For Daniel, our personal pick for right on
write-in!—J&W

Katie Kazoo, SWITCHEROO

Vote for ~~Katie~~ Suzanne

by Nancy Krulik • illustrated by John & Wendy

Grosset & Dunlap

Chapter 1

"Ooh, my stomach is killing me!" George Brennan groaned as he walked onto the school playground on Wednesday morning. He was holding his tummy with both hands.

"It's all those candy bars," Katie Carew told her friend.

"Not my fault," George insisted. "I got a ton of chocolate bars in my trick-or-treat bag."

"But no one said you had to eat them all last night," Suzanne Lock, Katie's best friend, pointed out.

George nodded. "I know, but they were so yummy!"

Katie knew exactly what he meant. It had been very hard to stop eating her Halloween candy. Especially the red licorice. That was her favorite.

"I miss Halloween already," Katie said with a sigh. She had really loved wearing her black cat costume. But now it was packed away in her costume box in the basement.

Katie looked around the playground. Just yesterday afternoon it had been filled with kids in costumes, all lined up for the school's Halloween parade.

Today, the kids were all in their normal clothes again. Bo-ring!

Well, *almost* all the kids were wearing their boring regular clothes. Suzanne was still wearing the crown from her fairy princess costume. She reached up and pressed a button on the crown. Bright pink lights began flashing on and off.

Katie giggled. That was such a Suzanne

thing to do. Her best friend really loved being the center of attention.

"I like that crown," Zoe Canter told Suzanne.

"It's so cool," Miriam Chan told Suzanne.

"It's so *yesterday*," George said, rolling his eyes.

"George, you can be such a jerk," Suzanne told him.

Katie shook her head. "He's right, Suzanne," she said. "It is so yesterday. Halloween *was* yesterday."

Suzanne didn't say anything. How could she argue with that?

The kids weren't focused on Suzanne's crown for long. A moment later, the bell rang. It was time to go into the school.

"I'll see you at lunch," Katie told Suzanne as the girls hurried into the building.

Suzanne nodded. "Definitely."

Katie watched Suzanne disappear into her classroom—4B. At the beginning of fourth

grade, Katie had felt bad about not being in the same class as her best friends, Suzanne and Jeremy. But now she was used to it.

Besides, being in class 4A was a lot of fun. There was always something interesting going on. Today was no exception.

"Good morning, Katie Kazoo," Mr. G. greeted Katie, using the way-cool nickname George had given her back in third grade.

Katie didn't answer. Instead she burst out laughing. She couldn't help it. Mr. G. looked so funny in his white wig and knee-length pants.

"You look like George Washington," Andy Epstein told Mr. G.

The teacher grinned. "That's who I am. I'm the first president."

"Is that your Halloween costume?" Kevin Camilleri asked.

Mr. G. shook his head. "Nope," he said. "I'm ready for another special day."

Some kids might be stunned to find their

teacher all dressed up like George Washington.
But the kids in 4A were never shocked by the
wacky things Mr. G. did. He was always full of
surprises.

"Wow! Look at this place!" Kadeem Carter exclaimed. "It's amazing."

Katie glanced around. Just yesterday, the classroom had been decorated with orange pumpkins and black cat posters. But today, everything had changed. The whole room was covered in red, white, and blue.

Fifty white stars were glued to a blue cloth taped to the ceiling. Thirteen streamers—seven red and six white—were hanging from the light fixture beneath the stars.

"It's like a giant 3-D American flag," Emma Weber pointed out.

"Exactly!" Mr. G. told her.

"But the Fourth of July isn't until *July*," Kevin told Mr. G. "Today is November first."

"Right. And President's Day isn't until February," Mr. G. explained. "Our new learning adventure is about something that's coming up next Tuesday. Does anyone know what that is?"

Katie raised her hand proudly. "It's Election Day!"

"Exactly," Mr. G. said. "Election Day is always on the first Tuesday in November. And this year is special, because here in Cherrydale we all get to vote to choose a mayor."

"Not everyone," Katie corrected Mr. G. "Kids aren't allowed to vote."

Mr. G. didn't answer. He just gave Katie a funny little smile. Then he turned to the rest of the class. "Hurry up and decorate your beanbag chairs, citizens," he said. "We've got a lot to do today."

Katie couldn't wait to get started. One of the best things about being in class 4A was that the kids got to sit in beanbag chairs instead of at desks. Mr. G. thought kids learned better when they were comfortable.

And the most fun thing about the beanbag chairs was decorating them every time a new learning adventure started! Katie ran over to the craft box and pulled out some silver foil and red and white construction paper. She was going to put stars and stripes all over her beanbag.

"Hey, Mr. G., do you know which president had the biggest family?" George called out to the teacher.

Mr. G. shook his head. "Which one?"

"George Washington. He's the father of our whole country!" George began to laugh at his own joke. The kids all laughed, too.

Now Kadeem had to get a joke in. "What do you get when you cross a gorilla with our sixteenth president?" he asked.

"What?" Mandy Banks wondered.

"Ape-raham Lincoln!" Kadeem exclaimed. Everyone started laughing all over again.

"Speaking of Abraham Lincoln," George butted in, "do you know why he wore that big black top hat?"

"Why?" Emma Stavros asked.

"To keep his head warm!" George laughed really hard at that one.

"Great! We've got an Election Day joke-off!" Mr. G. shouted happily. "Your turn, Kadeem."

"Do you know why George Washington slept standing up?" Kadeem asked the class.

"Why?" Kevin wondered.

"Because he couldn't lie," Kadeem answered.

Katie grinned and looked up at the giant flag on the ceiling. One thing she knew for sure. If there were elections for best teacher, Mr. G. would get her vote.

If kids could actually vote, that is.

Chapter 2

"We're like chimps in the zoo!" Jessica Haynes exclaimed as she flipped upside down on the monkey bars in the school playground at lunchtime.

"Ook, ook, ook!" Katie scratched her head and her armpit at the same time. That was her best upside-down monkey imitation.

Just then, Suzanne and Mandy walked by. When Suzanne saw her friends, she climbed on the monkey bars, too.

"I can't believe you're doing that wearing a dress," Mandy told Suzanne. "Everyone will see your underpants."

"Not a problem," Suzanne assured her. She lifted her skirt with one hand. "See, I've got shorts on underneath."

Katie grinned. Only Suzanne could have figured out a way to hang upside down in a dress.

But the girls didn't stay on the monkey bars very long. For one thing, after a while, hanging upside down gave Katie a headache. And for another, it was kind of boring.

"I am so sick of this playground," Jessica moaned as the girls climbed down and headed over toward the swings.

"I know," Mandy agreed. "We've been playing on the same swings, slide, and monkey bars since we were in kindergarten."

"We need new things, like those merry-go-rounds you spin around on until you throw up," Jessica suggested. "My cousin calls them vomit wheels."

Mandy made a face. "That's gross," she groaned.

"We could also use a rope swing," Jessica suggested instead.

"We *will* have all those things. Really, really soon!" Suzanne said with a smile.

Katie had seen that smile before. It was the one Suzanne got whenever she knew something no one else did.

"We will?" Jessica asked excitedly.

Suzanne nodded. "I read it in the newspaper this morning. They're building a new playground in that empty lot next to the Cherrydale Arena."

"Oh, wow!" Katie exclaimed. "A new playground!"

"Yep," Suzanne told her. "Good thing I'm grown-up enough to read the newspaper while I eat breakfast. Otherwise, you guys never would have known about it."

Mandy shook her head. "You're wrong, Suzanne," she said.

Those were words Suzanne never liked

hearing. "I am not wrong!" she exclaimed angrily. "I know what I read."

"Well, I know what I *heard*," Mandy told her. "And on the radio they said the mayor was thinking about putting a parking lot there."

"Okay, he might have *thought* about that," Suzanne argued. "But now he's putting in a playground instead."

"He is not," Mandy insisted.

"Mandy, I wish you would just be quiet!" Suzanne shouted.

Katie gulped. Suzanne had just made a wish. That could be really bad.

"You do not wish that!" she exclaimed suddenly. "You do not wish anything!"

Suzanne, Mandy, and Jessica all stared at her.

Katie knew her friends thought she'd gone bananas—maybe from hanging on the monkey bars too long. But Katie wasn't bananas, or nuts for that matter. She had a really good reason for being afraid of wishes.

It had all started one horrible day back in third grade. Katie had lost the football game for her team. Then she'd splashed mud all over her favorite jeans. But the worst part of the day came when Katie let out a loud burp— right in front of the whole class. Talk about embarrassing!

That night, Katie wished to be anyone but herself. There must have been a shooting star overhead when she made the wish, because the very next day the magic wind came.

The magic wind was like a really powerful tornado that blew only around Katie. It was so strong, it could blow her right out of her body . . . *and into someone else's!*

The first time the magic wind appeared, it turned Katie into Speedy, the hamster in her third-grade class. Katie spent the whole morning going round and round on a hamster wheel and chewing on Speedy's wooden chew sticks. Those tasted terrible.

But being caged up wasn't even the worst part. Things got *really* bad when she escaped from Speedy's cage and ran into the boys' locker room. That was when Katie landed inside George Brennan's stinky sneaker! *P.U.!* Katie sure was glad when the magic wind came back and switcherooed her into herself again!

Another time, the magic wind had turned Katie into Suzanne—right in the middle of a fashion show. Katie wound up putting on Suzanne's pants backward and falling in her high heels. What a disaster! Suzanne had been so embarrassed—and confused. After all, she wasn't sure how any of it had happened. Which kind of made sense, since it had been Katie up there on the runway—not her.

The magic wind didn't stop there. It just kept

coming and coming. Just a few weeks ago, when the kids were on a field trip to the aquarium, the magic wind had changed Katie into a clown fish. She wound up swimming around in a tank filled with big *sharks*! Talk about a scary switcheroo!

Katie never knew when the magic wind would come and cause more trouble. She just knew that sooner or later it would be back. And it was all because of the wish she'd made.

That was why Katie hated when anyone made any kind of wish. But of course Katie couldn't tell her friends about the magic wind and its switcheroos. They wouldn't believe her even if she did. Katie wouldn't have believed it, either, if it didn't keep happening to her.

Still, she had to say *something*. They were all staring at her. "I just meant you guys don't have to fight over this," she told her friends quickly.

"Exactly," Mandy agreed. "Because the man on the radio said there's going to be a parking lot," she insisted.

"You must have heard wrong," Suzanne told her.

Mandy shook her head. "My ears work just fine."

"They should," Suzanne told her. "They're big enough."

Mandy got really mad at that. Her face turned beet red. "Oh yeah?" she demanded. "Well, your hair is all messed up from hanging upside down."

"Well, your . . ." Suzanne began.

Before she could finish her sentence, Mr. G. came running over to stop the argument. "What's the deal?" he asked the girls.

"Do you know if there's going to be a new playground in that empty lot near the Cherrydale Arena?" Suzanne asked.

"Or a parking garage?" Mandy asked him.

"*That's* what you're fighting over?" Mr. G. asked.

Mandy and Suzanne both looked down at the ground. They seemed sort of embarrassed.

Katie didn't blame them. It was kind of a dumb thing to argue over.

"We weren't fighting, exactly," Suzanne murmured.

"Good," Mr. G. said. "Because fighting doesn't solve anything. Besides, I know where you can get the answer to that question. You can ask Mayor Fogelhymer."

"Great idea! Let's call and ask him!" Katie exclaimed. "Do you have the mayor's phone number, Mr. G.?"

Mr. G. smiled. "I can do better than that. You can ask the mayor that question in person."

"How?" the girls all asked at once.

"He's coming to school today for a special fourth-grade assembly," Mr. G. explained. "It was supposed to be a surprise. Mayor

Fogelhymer is going to talk to you dudes about Election Day."

Katie's eyes opened wide. She couldn't believe she was going to get to meet someone as important as the mayor of Cherrydale.

"Well, I'm definitely going to ask him about the playground," Suzanne said.

"And *I'm* going to ask him about the parking lot," Mandy said.

Katie knew Suzanne was going to brag a lot if the mayor said she was right and Mandy was wrong. That's what she always did.

But this time Katie didn't care. She really hoped Suzanne was right. A playground was so much more important than a dumb old parking lot. Everyone could see that.

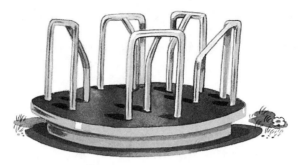

Chapter 3

Well, maybe not *everyone*.

Katie could tell that Mayor Fogelhymer was pretty uncomfortable with all the questions the fourth-graders were asking during the assembly.

"Don't you think kids need a playground?" Jeremy Fox asked the mayor.

"Well, um, of course they do," Mayor Fogelhymer stammered. "But a lot of you already have swings and things in your backyards."

"I don't," Katie shouted out.

"Me neither," Suzanne agreed.

"I have a tire swing and a slide at my house," Jessica said. "But I don't have a vomit wheel."

The kids all started to laugh.

Katie looked around the room. Not only was the mayor at her school, but a whole lot of reporters and cameramen were there, too. Mayor Fogelhymer's visit to the local elementary school was a big news event. How cool was that?

Mayor Fogelhymer didn't seem to think his visit was too cool. In fact, he seemed kind of sorry he'd ever come to Cherrydale Elementary School.

"Well, you have a wonderful playground here at school," Mayor Fogelhymer said.

"Don't you like kids?" Emma W. asked the mayor.

"Of course I do," Mayor Fogelhymer assured her.

"Then why do you want to put up a parking

lot there now?" Zoe asked him.

"You know, there are a lot of cars in Cherrydale," the mayor told them.

"There are a lot of kids, too!" Suzanne exclaimed.

"Yeah!" Katie cheered along with the other fourth-graders.

Mayor Fogelhymer took out a handkerchief and wiped away little beads of sweat that had formed on his forehead.

The news photographers clicked pictures of the sweaty mayor.

"Well, I have not made a final decision about the empty lot. So we may as well move on," Mayor Fogelhymer told the kids. "Now, does anyone else have anything to ask about Election Day? After all, that's what I came here to talk about."

None of the fourth-graders had any more questions for the mayor. But Ms. Sweet, the teacher in class 4B, did.

"What made you want to run for mayor?" she asked.

Mayor Fogelhymer smiled at her. "Now that's the kind of question I like to answer. I wanted to be mayor of Cherrydale because I love this town and I care about the people who live here. I wanted to make things better for all of us. And I think I have."

"We'd be better off if we had a new playground," Suzanne said in a loud whisper.

Mayor Fogelhymer pretended not to hear. Instead, he smiled right into the cameras. "I want to be the one to *keep* the people of Cherrydale happy. Kids, I hope all of your parents will vote for me on Tuesday. That way I can be mayor for another four years!"

Andy raised his hand.

"Yes?" the mayor asked him.

"Who are you running against?" he wondered.

"A man named Sam Barth," Mayor

Fogelhymer told him. "It's his first election. He has never held any public office. I don't think he realizes how much work is involved in this job."

"Well, we'll be able to ask him about that," Mr. G. said. "He's coming here tomorrow to talk to our students."

Mayor Fogelhymer frowned. He didn't seem too happy about that.

A few minutes later, the mayor said good-bye to the kids. As he walked out of the auditorium, the crowd of reporters and photographers followed.

As soon as the mayor was gone, Mandy leaned over and said to Suzanne, "See, I told you so."

"He didn't say for sure that there would be a parking lot there," Suzanne insisted.

"He didn't say there would be a playground, either," Mandy pointed out.

"He didn't really say *anything*," Jeremy told the girls.

Katie frowned. That was the truth. Mayor Fogelhymer's visit had been very disappointing.

"I don't know why he didn't just tell us that he would make the playground," George said. "He said he wanted to make the people of Cherrydale happy. That would make me happy."

"Me too," Suzanne said.

"If *I* were mayor, I'd build a new playground," Katie added.

"You'd be a better mayor than Mayor Fogelhymer, Katie Kazoo," George told her.

"Well, maybe Katie will get the chance to find out just what kind of mayor she would be." Mr. G. smiled mysteriously as he interrupted the kids' conversation.

Huh? Katie and her friends all looked curiously at the teacher.

"We're going to have our own election," Mr. G. explained.

"You're going to be electing your own fourth-grade mayor," Ms. Sweet added.

Katie's eyes opened wide. Now *this* was exciting!

"Each class will nominate two people to run for mayor," Mr. G. explained. "The four candidates will campaign for the rest of this week. School will be closed on Election Day. So, next Monday, we'll have *our* Election Day."

Katie looked around the room at all of her classmates. By this time next week, one of them would be the mayor of the fourth grade.

Who would it be?

Chapter 4

"Mom!" Katie screamed as she raced into the house after school. "You won't believe it."

"What's all the excitement about?" Mrs. Carew asked as she hurried to the front hall.

"I'm running for mayor!" Katie squealed excitedly.

Mrs. Carew looked confused.

"Of the fourth grade," Katie explained.

"Oh," Mrs. Carew said. "That *is* exciting."

"It sure is," Katie agreed. "Andy Epstein is running, too. He's the other nominee from class 4A. Each class has two nominees."

"Who's been nominated from class 4B?"

Katie's mom asked her.

Katie stopped for a minute and thought. "I don't know," she admitted. "I was so excited to tell you that I didn't wait around after school to ask."

Mrs. Carew laughed. "Well, I'm sure you'll find out soon enough," she said.

"George and Emma W. are my campaign managers," Katie told her mother. "They're coming over after I get home from my Cooking Class. They promised to help me make posters and stuff."

"Great!" Katie's mom replied. "We have lots of poster board, markers, and glitter glue in the basement."

"Perfect!" Katie exclaimed.

Rrringg. Just then, the phone rang.

"I'll get it!" Katie shouted as she ran to pick up the telephone. "Hello."

"Hi, Katie. It's me, Suzanne."

"Hi," Katie said. "You won't believe—"

Suzanne didn't let Katie finish her sentence. Instead, she asked, "You're going to vote for me, right?"

"Huh?" Katie asked, surprised.

"For mayor," Suzanne explained. "My class nominated me to run. And I know I can count on you to vote for me because we're best friends."

Uh-oh. Katie's eyes flew open wide.

"Well, I really *can't* vote for you, Suzanne," Katie said slowly.

"Why not?" Suzanne demanded. "I'd vote for you if *you* were running for mayor."

"I *am* running," Katie explained.

Suzanne was quiet for a minute. Then she said, "But you can't run, Katie."

"Why not?" Katie asked her.

"Well . . . it's just that I don't want you to get hurt," Suzanne said.

"Hurt?" Katie was confused.

"You're going to feel just awful when I win

and you lose," Suzanne said. "You're my best friend. I want to protect you from that."

Suzanne was using her super-sweet voice. It was the one she used when she was saying something mean, but she wanted to sound nice. That voice always made Katie mad.

"Who says *you'll* win?" Katie asked her.

"Don't be silly," Suzanne replied. "I'm the best candidate for mayor. No one will look better on posters and in photos than I do. I'm a model."

"You take modeling *classes*," Katie corrected her. "And besides, what does that have to do with being mayor?"

"You saw all the news photographers following Mayor Fogelhymer today," Suzanne explained. "A mayor always has to be ready for her close-up."

"A mayor has to be ready to help the people in her class," Katie corrected Suzanne.

"That too," Suzanne muttered. "Anyway, run

if you want to. Just don't come crying to me when you lose."

"Whatever," Katie said with a sigh. "May the best fourth-grader win."

"Oh, I will," Suzanne said.

Katie frowned as she hung up the phone. Suzanne had been really awful to her. And Katie had a feeling she wasn't finished being mean, either. Still, Katie wasn't going to give up.

Suzanne doesn't scare me, she thought. *Well, not that much, anyway.*

Chapter 5

Katie arrived at school on Thursday morning with her campaign posters. She walked into the school cafeteria and began hanging them on the walls.

Katie's posters were all really nice. She, Emma W., and George had worked on them for a long time last night. They were colorful and glittery. And each one had a different saying.

The poster George had made had a big photo of Katie glued to it. Under her picture he had written, VOTE FOR KATIE KAZOO! SHE'LL WORK FOR YOU!

Emma W.'s had a big clock on it. It said, IT'S KATIE TIME!

Katie had drawn a picture of Pepper, her cocker spaniel, on a poster. Then she had written, THIS DOG'S BEST FRIEND IS *YOUR* BEST FRIEND. VOTE KATIE FOR MAYOR!

Manny Gonzalez was already in the cafeteria hanging his posters when Katie arrived. He was the other nominee from Suzanne's class.

Manny's posters were kind of cool. He'd used his computer to print out pictures of his head on Mayor Fogelhymer's body. Then he had written, THE FUTURE MAYOR.

"Hi, Katie," Manny greeted her. "I didn't know you were running for mayor."

Katie nodded. "Our class picked Andy and me."

"Suzanne is the other person running from our class," Manny said.

"I heard," Katie said with a frown. She taped

one of her posters to the wall.

A moment later, Andy walked into the cafeteria. He only had one poster. But it was huge. Andy had used a whole roll of white wrapping paper for his poster. On the paper, he had written, A IS FOR ACTION. A IS FOR ACHIEVEMENT. A IS FOR ANDREW. GET STRAIGHT AS. VOTE FOR ANDREW!

Katie had to admit that was kind of cool.

"I wonder where Suzanne is?" Manny said. "She hasn't put up her posters yet."

Katie had been thinking the same thing. But she really didn't want to see Suzanne. Not after their conversation last night.

Still, there was no way Katie could avoid Suzanne forever. In fact, a few minutes later, she came storming into the cafeteria.

"Katie! You are such a copycat!" Suzanne shouted angrily.

"What are you talking about?" Katie asked her.

"You put glitter on your posters!" Suzanne explained angrily.

"So what?" Katie wondered.

"Glitter is my thing!" Suzanne insisted. "I was going to put glitter all over my posters. You stole that idea!"

"How could I have stolen your idea if I didn't know you were doing that?" Katie pointed out.

"You knew I would be putting glitter on my posters," Suzanne went on. "I always wear glitter. Glitter earrings. Glitter pins. Glitter shirts. You hardly ever wear glitter."

Katie looked at Suzanne. Today, she was wearing a glitter clip in her hair and a blue and white glittery T-shirt. But that didn't mean anything.

"You don't own glitter," Katie told Suzanne firmly.

Suzanne's eyes closed into little angry slits.

"Suzanne, aren't you going to put up any posters?" Andy asked her.

"Yeah, where are your posters, anyway?" Katie wondered.

Suzanne shook her head. "I haven't made my posters yet. I spent last night making something much better."

"What?" Katie asked her.

"I'm not telling you," Suzanne replied. "You're the enemy."

Katie could feel salty tears welling up in her eyes. Just yesterday morning, Suzanne had been her best friend. Now she was calling Katie her enemy. And keeping secrets from her, too.

Katie turned away so Suzanne couldn't see her tears. If she did, Suzanne would probably say that Katie was too much of a crybaby to be mayor.

Katie figured mayors didn't cry.

Not even fourth-grade mayors.

Chapter 6

By lunchtime, Suzanne's secret was out.

When the kids in class 4B arrived in the cafeteria, most of them were wearing huge red, white, and blue glittery buttons. The buttons said, LOCK ROCKS!

Katie sighed. Her glittery posters didn't seem so special anymore. Once again, Suzanne had managed to get everyone's attention.

And speaking of posters, Manny Gonzalez's were no longer hanging on the cafeteria walls.

"What happened to your posters?" Katie asked him.

"I'm not running for fourth-grade mayor anymore," Manny told her.

"Why not?" Katie wondered.

"I didn't think I could win," he told Katie.

"Why not?" she repeated.

"Well, Suzanne convinced me that she was a better candidate," Manny explained. "So I'm going to help her now."

Katie looked curiously at Manny. "*How* did Suzanne convince you?" she asked.

Manny looked down at the floor. "She kind of promised to get me a copy of Space Raiders if I decided not to run against her."

"Space Raiders?" Katie wondered. "That old computer game?"

"It's unbelievably awesome," Manny replied. "They don't make it anymore, so it's almost impossible to get."

"Then how is Suzanne going to get it for you?" Katie wondered.

Just then Suzanne walked over and stood

next to Manny. "My dad has a copy of Space Raiders. I'm going to give it to Manny."

"Your father won't let you give away his computer games," Katie told Suzanne.

"Sure he will," Suzanne insisted. "He told me he'd do whatever he could to help me get elected."

Katie didn't know what to say to that. So she just walked away and sat down next to George and Emma W. She wanted to be near people who were on her side.

"Can you guys come over tonight and help me write my speech?" she asked them. "All the candidates have to give their speeches next Monday, and I want to be able to practice mine over the weekend."

"Sure, Katie," Emma W. said. "I have some really good ideas."

George didn't say anything.

"How about you, George?" Katie asked him. "I could use some funny jokes in my speech."

George's face turned beet red. "I . . . um . . . I . . . well, I can't help you," he stammered.

"Why not?" Katie wondered.

"Well, I kind of promised I would help Suzanne write *her* speech," George admitted.

"Suzanne?" Katie was very surprised. George and Suzanne weren't friends at all. "I thought you were my campaign manager."

"I was," George began. "But . . ."

Just then, Suzanne came over and wrapped her arm around George's shoulders.

"Katie, I see you are talking to *my* new speechwriter," she said.

Katie couldn't believe her ears. "George! Why would you want to help Suzanne with her speech?" she asked.

"She promised to give me all of her Halloween candy if I did," George explained.

"Suzanne, that's cheating!" Katie exclaimed.

"No, it's not. It's politics." Suzanne smiled and walked away.

Katie wasn't really sure what Suzanne meant by that. But if it was true, Katie was certain of one thing.

Politics really stunk!

🌟 🌟 🌟

After lunch, the kids all herded back into the auditorium. This time, Sam Barth had come to talk to the kids. There were reporters following him, too.

Mayor Fogelhymer had seemed happy to have the reporters around him—at least most of the time he was talking. But Sam Barth didn't seem to like them at all. In fact, they seemed to make him kind of nervous. He was twirling a lock of hair around his finger. That was the same thing Katie did whenever *she* was nervous.

Sam Barth was a lot younger than Mayor Fogelhymer. And he wasn't wearing a suit like the mayor had been. He was wearing a pair of slacks and a button-down shirt with a tie.

Mr. G. climbed the stairs to the stage and stood next to Sam Barth. The kids grew quiet and got ready to listen to their teacher.

"Okay, dudes, as you know, in an election there are at least two candidates to choose from," Mr. G. told them. "You've already heard from Mayor Fogelhymer. Now it's time for you to hear what the other candidate for mayor has to say. It's important for people to hear both candidates' ideas before they vote. Does anyone have any questions for Mr. Barth?"

A sea of hands shot up in the air. Suzanne stood up in her chair so Sam Barth could see her.

Katie stood up, too. If Suzanne was going to get to ask a question, then she wanted to, too.

"Ooh, ooh," Suzanne called out. "Mr. Barth, I have a question."

"Me too," Katie said.

But Mr. Barth didn't call on Katie or Suzanne. He pointed to Jeremy instead.

Jeremy smiled and stood up to ask his question. "If you get to be mayor, will you put a parking garage or a playground in that empty lot?" he asked.

Mr. Barth frowned. He went back to twirling his hair around his finger. "The empty lot?" he asked nervously.

"Yeah," Jeremy replied. "You know, the one near the arena?"

"Oh, that lot," Mr. Barth said. "Well, that's

a tough question. You see, there are a lot of things to think about. I would have to look at a lot of information and . . ."

Katie sighed. Sam Barth wasn't giving the kids a straight answer. He was just talking a lot and not saying anything—just like Mayor Fogelhymer.

Was there any difference between them?

✴ ✴ ✴

Suzanne could tell the difference. And she'd already picked who she thought would be the winner.

"Mayor Fogelhymer is going to win the election," she told the kids as they left the school building that afternoon.

"How can you tell?" Miriam asked her.

"He wore a suit," Suzanne said.

"So? Does that matter?" Katie wondered.

Suzanne rolled her eyes. "Katie, that's why you will never be our mayor. A candidate's clothes are very important. Mayor Fogelhymer looked much more professional in his suit."

Katie looked down at her pink sweater and running pants. She didn't look like a mayor. But Suzanne's glittery shirt and jeans didn't look like something a mayor would wear, either.

Katie decided she would have to say something important in her speech. Yes! Something that sounded very mayor-like. Something that would make all the kids want to vote for her.

Katie frowned. She had no idea what that could be.

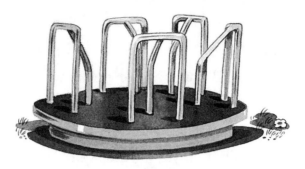

Chapter 7

"Thanks for helping me with my speech, you guys," Katie told Jeremy and Emma W. later that afternoon. "I'm glad some people are still behind me."

"Lots of kids want you to win," Emma W. assured Katie. She looked at the computer screen in front of her. "Your speech is going to be great."

"I could never vote for Suzanne," Jeremy told Katie. "She's bossy enough as it is. She'll be impossible if she's mayor."

"You're not kidding," Emma W. agreed. "You remember that time she got a bunch of us to garden with her?"

Katie giggled. "How could I forget?" she said. "She called gardening the War of the Roses. She named herself the general."

"And we were all soldiers in her army," Emma W. recalled. She made a face. "She even ordered us to put stinky rotten fish all around the rosebushes."

Jeremy shook his head. "I'm glad you're never mean like Suzanne is, Katie."

"I try not to be," Katie told him.

"That's why people will vote for you," Emma W. said. "They're just helping Suzanne right now because she bribed them. But soon they'll see through her."

"I sure hope so," Katie said. "I'll bet Andy hopes so, too."

"Who's helping him with his speech?" Jeremy asked.

Katie shrugged. "I don't know," she admitted. "He doesn't talk about the election too much. He had a nice poster, though."

"Let's stop worrying about what Andy and Suzanne are going to say," Emma W. said. "We've got a speech to write. We have to tell the kids why you're better than Andy and Suzanne are."

"Exactly," Jeremy agreed. "Do you have any stories about Suzanne that could make her look bad?"

"Shouldn't I be telling kids things that make *me* look *good*?" Katie asked him.

"Sure," Jeremy said. "But it would help if we could make Suzanne look bad, too."

Katie thought for a minute. She knew a lot of secrets about Suzanne. Things her friend would never want anyone else to know. Like the fact that she was scared of spiders and the dark. Or that she wasn't very good at spelling. And that she wore a night brace on her teeth.

But Katie couldn't say those things in her speech. Those were secrets between her and

Suzanne. And no matter how mad Suzanne made her, Katie could never tell them to anyone.

"No, there aren't any stories I could tell," Katie told her friends.

"I'll bet there are," Jeremy said. "You're just too nice."

"That's it!" Katie exclaimed suddenly. "I'll be the nice candidate."

"The what?" Emma W. and Jeremy asked at one time.

"The nice candidate," Katie repeated. "I'll talk about how nice I am. Being nice is important because a mayor has to be nice to get along with everyone. That will make people vote for me."

⋆ ⋆ ⋆

Katie didn't have to worry about Suzanne copying her. Suzanne didn't want to be a nice candidate. Not at all!

The next morning, as Katie walked onto the

playground, she overheard Suzanne talking to a group of kids. She was saying some pretty awful things.

"You can't vote for Katie," Suzanne told them. "She's a big baby. Do you know once during a sleepover she peed in the bed? My mom had to get up in the middle of the night to change the sheets and give her a pair of my dry pajamas!"

Katie's face turned beet red. That had been all the way back in first grade! Three whole years ago!

But Suzanne hadn't told the kids that part. She'd made it sound like it happened just last week!

Katie thought about telling the kids the truth, but she was too embarrassed to even look at them. So instead, she ran into the cafeteria. She was hoping to be alone for a minute.

The first thing Katie spotted when she walked into the cafeteria was a new poster. It was Suzanne's.

Katie hated to admit it, but the poster was really cool. Someone had used a computer to put Suzanne into pictures with George Washington and Abraham Lincoln. Underneath the pictures it said, GREAT AMERICAN LEADERS.

Katie sighed. There was only one person in the whole fourth grade who knew enough about computers to make a poster like that. Manny Gonzalez. No wonder Suzanne had wanted him to be on her team.

Still, Katie liked her own posters best. She looked over at the wall where they were hanging.

Oh, no! Someone had drawn a mustache and a beard on the one with Katie's photo on it. The poster was ruined!

And so was the poster that said, IT'S KATIE TIME. Someone had changed it. Now it said, IT'S NOT KATIE TIME!

Grrr.

There was only one person in the world
mean enough to do that!

Suddenly, Katie was mad.

Madder than she'd ever been.

So mad that she did something she never thought she would.

Katie spilled one of Suzanne's secrets.

Quickly, she reached into her backpack and pulled out a black Magic Marker. Then she walked over to Suzanne's poster and drew a big, ugly night brace across Suzanne's smiling mouth!

Chapter 8

When lunchtime came, Katie took her tray and sat down beside Jeremy. When Suzanne got her food, she went to sit at the other end of the table, with Jessica. It felt kind of weird not to be sitting near Suzanne, but Katie wasn't going to move. She knew Suzanne wouldn't, either.

Just then, Miriam stormed over to Suzanne. "I didn't know you wore a night brace," she said.

Suzanne looked up at her, surprised.

"W-what?" she asked nervously.

"You made me feel so bad when I got my

braces," Miriam shouted at Suzanne. "You told me braces were ugly. And all that time, you're sleeping in a night brace!"

Suzanne got all embarrassed. "How did you know about that?" she asked.

Miriam pointed to Suzanne's poster. "It's right there," she said.

Suzanne's eyes grew wide as she spotted what Katie had drawn on her Great Leaders poster.

Katie gulped. When Suzanne got angry, you
never knew *what* could happen.

"Katie Carew, you are such a creep!"
Suzanne exclaimed. "That was supposed to be
a secret!"

Katie turned bright red.

"I'm glad Katie let everyone know about your night brace," Miriam told Suzanne. "Now we all know what a faker you are! I wouldn't vote for you if you were the only person running for mayor!"

By now, the whole fourth grade was staring at Miriam and Suzanne. Everyone had heard what Miriam had said. From the looks on their faces, Katie could tell lots of other kids had decided not to vote for Suzanne, either.

Suddenly, Katie felt sort of creepy. The night brace *had* been a secret. Katie shouldn't have done what she did, even if Suzanne had blabbed about Katie wetting the bed. How many times had her parents said that two wrongs didn't make a right?

"Miriam, think about it," Suzanne urged. "You can't vote for Katie. She's scared of everything. And she gets carsick. Remember that field trip we took to the fire station? She threw up all over the bus!"

Katie frowned. "That was in kindergarten!" she shouted.

"It could happen again," Suzanne continued. "Who wants a mayor who will throw up in the car on the way to a ribbon-cutting ceremony or a big fancy ball?"

"Fourth-grade mayors don't cut ribbons or go to fancy balls," Jeremy reminded Suzanne.

Katie looked up and smiled gratefully. Jeremy smiled back at her.

Just then, Mr. G. raced over. "What's all the commotion, dudes?" he asked. "I can hear you all the way at the teachers' table."

"Suzanne said I shouldn't be mayor because I got carsick one time!" Katie complained.

"Yeah, well, you told everyone about my night brace," Suzanne snapped back.

"Only because . . ." Katie began.

"Whoa, hold on," Mr. G. told the girls. "This is no way to run a campaign. It's not a popularity contest. It's an *election*. You should be telling the people what you would do to make their lives better. Let them know why they should vote *for* you. Not why they should vote *against* the other person."

"Oooh," George moaned suddenly. He bent over.

Everyone turned to look at him.

"Are you okay?" Kevin asked him.

George shook his head. "I have a bad stomachache."

"It's all that candy you've been eating," Mandy said. She pointed to George's tray. There were candy bar wrappers all over it.

"Oooh," George moaned again.

"You'd better go to the nurse," Emma S. told him.

"I'll take you, George," Mr. G. said. He hurried over and helped George out of his seat.

"Poor George," Katie said quietly. Then she turned to Suzanne. "It's all your fault."

"*My* fault?" Suzanne exclaimed.

"You gave him all of your Halloween candy," Katie explained. "If you hadn't bribed him to be on your side, he wouldn't be sick now."

"I don't need to bribe anyone," Suzanne told Katie. "People can just spot a winner."

Katie frowned. She understood what Mr. G. had said. But her teacher didn't know how mean Suzanne could be. And he didn't realize how angry that made Katie feel.

"They sure can spot a winner," Katie said. "And it's not you!"

Suzanne stared at Katie with surprise.

Katie was surprised, too. She never said mean stuff like that. But somehow this whole election thing was changing her. For a minute, she thought about dropping out of the race before things got any worse between her and Suzanne.

But then Katie heard Suzanne say, "You guys can't vote for Katie. We can't have a copycat, secret-telling baby for our mayor. We have to have someone cool. We have to have me!"

"I'm not a baby! I'm three months older than *you*!" Katie shouted at Suzanne. "And if you think saying mean things is going to make me drop out of this race, you're wrong! I'm going to keep on running. And I'm going to win!"

Chapter 9

Katie was really glad when lunch and recess were over. Mr. G. didn't let the kids talk about the election inside their classroom. He said that their classroom was a campaign-free zone.

Katie was sick and tired of fighting over who would become mayor of the fourth grade. She was glad to just focus on her schoolwork.

Mr. G. told the class, "We're going to be doing oral reports on the presidents of the United States. I want you each to choose a president. Then write your choice on a piece of paper and hand it in to me."

Katie thought about that for a minute. She remembered her grandmother telling her about Harry Truman. He had been president back when her grandmother was born.

Katie thought it would be kind of cool to do her report about him. So she tore a piece of paper from her notebook and wrote: *Katie Kazoo → Harry Truman.*

Just as Katie was writing the letter *n*, George shouted out, "I want to do my report on John F. Kennedy."

"No fair!" Kadeem exclaimed. "That's who I wanted."

"I said it first," George told Kadeem.

"You're not supposed to say it," Kadeem replied. "You're supposed to write it down on a piece of paper."

"Yeah, well, I'm still going to do my report on John F. Kennedy," George insisted.

"Wanna bet?" Kadeem shouted.

Katie gulped. Oh, no. More fighting.

Mr. G. jumped in. "Dudes, you don't have to argue about this," he told the boys.

"Yes, we do," Kadeem insisted. "Because I'm not going to let him steal my president."

"*Your* president?" George growled. "Since when is John F. Kennedy *your* president?"

"Dudes, relax," Mr. G. said. "You can both do your reports on John F. Kennedy."

"But we're doing oral reports. That means we're supposed to *talk* about our presidents," George pointed out. "Kadeem's report will seem pretty boring after mine."

"My report will not be boring!" Kadeem insisted. "And who says you're going first?"

"You don't have to do the same report," Mr. G. told the boys. "You can compromise."

"How?" George asked.

"You'll do your report about John F. Kennedy's childhood," Mr. G. told George. "And Kadeem, you can talk about what he was like as an adult."

George and Kadeem looked at each other.

"I guess it's okay," Kadeem mumbled.

"Yeah, sure," George agreed.

"Good." Mr. G. smiled. "I'm glad you agreed to compromise. Now, if the rest of you will hand in your slips of paper, we can go down to the library and get started on our research."

* * *

Katie loved working in the library. It was fun to sit at a big table with lots of books around her, taking notes about an interesting subject. Right now, reading about President Truman playing the piano made Katie forget all the things Suzanne had said about her.

But once the bell rang and the school day was over, Katie's good mood vanished. She took her time packing up her things. What if the other kids made fun of her for throwing up on the bus in kindergarten or wetting the bed in first grade?

Slowly, Katie walked out of the school building.

A bunch of fourth-graders were gathered on the street. They were talking to Mandy's mom. They all looked too upset to think about the school election.

What was going on?

"I can't believe Mayor Fogelhymer said okay to a parking garage on that big empty lot," Mandy groaned.

"I'm afraid it's true," her mom told the kids. "I just heard it on the car radio. And this time it's definite. The mayor is meeting with the garage builders tomorrow."

"Well, that's that." Kevin groaned. "No new playground."

"Not necessarily," Andy piped up. "We can still do something about it."

"What?" Mandy asked. "We're just kids."

"When I was doing research on President Wilson," Andy explained, "I saw all these pictures of women protesting in front of the White House."

"You mean, like, with signs and stuff?" George asked. "What were they doing that for?"

"It was a real long time ago," Andy explained. "Back then, women weren't allowed to vote. That made them really mad. So they started carrying signs and protesting about how mean it was that they weren't part of an election. And the protests worked. In 1920, women got the right to vote."

"We could make protest signs and march around City Hall!" Katie exclaimed excitedly.

"What a wonderful idea!" Mrs. Banks exclaimed. "You kids should really stand up for what you believe in."

"We could go to City Hall tomorrow," Jeremy suggested. "It's Saturday, so we don't have school."

"I'm going to go home and start making

signs right now," Andy said.

"I'll help you," Zoe told him.

Suzanne turned and smiled triumphantly at Mandy. "See? I told you it wasn't over. We still might get our playground. And when we do, I will have been right and you will have been wrong."

Mandy rolled her eyes. "Whatever," she said. "I don't care, as long as we get our playground."

"We will," Suzanne told Mandy. Then she turned and stared right at Katie. "I always get what I want."

Katie didn't answer. She was too focused on Saturday to fight with Suzanne. It was exciting to protest.

Mayor Fogelhymer had better watch out. The fourth grade was coming to City Hall!

Chapter 10

By nine-thirty Saturday morning, there was a big crowd of kids outside City Hall. And not just fourth-graders, either. There were kids of all ages and grown-ups, too. Just about everyone at Cherrydale Elementary School had heard about the protest and wanted the mayor to know how they felt about the new playground!

Katie and Jeremy were in the crowd, carrying their signs.

Katie's said, PLAYGROUNDS ARE HEALTHY FOR CHILDREN!

Jeremy's sign said, SWINGS YES! CARS NO!

"I don't see any news cameras or reporters," Jeremy pointed out. He sounded worried.

"They'll be here as soon as Mayor Fogelhymer arrives," Katie assured him.

"What if the mayor doesn't work on Saturday?"

"He'll be here," Katie told him. "On the radio, they said he was meeting with some people from the garage company at ten o'clock."

"Jeremy, over here!" Becky Stern called out from the other side of the steps.

Jeremy sighed. "Oh, man," he groaned.

Katie felt bad for Jeremy. Becky was always flirting with him. She had a big crush on him. Jeremy, however, did not have a crush on Becky.

"We can't leave," Katie told Jeremy. "We have to fight for the playground."

Jeremy nodded. "You're right."

Katie scanned the crowd. Over toward the left, closest to the City Hall steps, she spotted Suzanne. Ordinarily, Katie would have shouted and waved to her. But not today.

As for Suzanne, every now and then she glanced over to where Katie and Jeremy were standing. But she would turn away quickly as soon as her eyes met Katie's.

Suddenly, a long black car pulled up to the curb. Two news vans followed close behind.

"He's here!" Mandy shouted out. "It's Mayor Fogelhymer!"

As the mayor got out of his car, the kids all began to chant. "One, two, three, four! We want swings and slides and more!"

The news reporters leaped out of their vans. Cameramen began to film the protesting kids.

As soon as the cameras appeared, Suzanne started jumping up and down in the air, waving her arms like a cheerleader.

"One, two, three, four!" Suzanne shouted. "We want swings and slides and more!"

As she said the word *more,* Suzanne reached out her arms and began to do a cartwheel. But she tripped over her open shoelace.

Bam! Suzanne landed right on her rear end.

"I can't wait to see *that* on the evening news," Jeremy joked.

Normally, Katie wouldn't have liked hearing Jeremy make fun of Suzanne. But right now, Suzanne *wasn't* her best friend. She was the person Katie was running against. After all,

Suzanne had decided that Katie was her enemy. So Katie laughed along with everyone else.

Mayor Fogelhymer began walking up the steps of City Hall.

"One, two, three, four," the kids chanted at him. "We want swings and slides and more!"

The mayor didn't even glance at the chanting crowd.

"Why do you hate kids?" Katie asked the mayor as he passed by.

Mayor Fogelhymer stopped, turned, and stared at her. "Me? I *like* kids. That's not fair to say," he said. Then he gave the cameras a tight, fake smile.

A few moments later, Emma W. came running over to Katie and Jeremy. "Sorry I'm late," she said. "I had to watch the twins until my mom and dad got back from the store. Did I miss anything?"

Jeremy shook his head.

"But we're not giving up!" Katie exclaimed.

She raised her sign even higher.

"Are there any more protest signs?" Emma W. asked. "I didn't get a chance to make one last night."

Katie nodded. "Andy, Kadeem, and Zoe made extras," she said. "They left them in a pile on the other side of the building."

"Where?" Emma W. asked.

Katie handed Emma W. the sign she had been carrying. "Here, you take mine," she told her friend. "I'll go get another one."

And with that, Katie hurried off.

Katie could still hear the chanting from the far side of the building. She spotted the signs leaning against the stone wall. As she hurried over, Katie felt a cool breeze blowing on the back of her neck. That was funny. It had been really warm out a minute ago.

The breeze suddenly grew stronger, blowing hard and cold against Katie's back—*and nowhere else.* Not in the trees. Not in the grass.

Not in the clouds. They were all completely still.

Katie gulped. That could mean only one thing.

This was no ordinary wind. This was the magic wind!

"Oh, no! Not now!" Katie cried out.

But there was no stopping the magic wind. The cold wind began to circle faster and faster around Katie! In a flash, the tornado was whirling wildly, blowing Katie's bright red hair all over her face. She closed her eyes and tried not to cry. The magic wind was so strong that Katie was sure it was going to blow her away.

And then it stopped. Just like that. The magic wind was gone.

So was Katie Kazoo.

She'd turned into someone else . . . one, two, switcheroo!

But who?

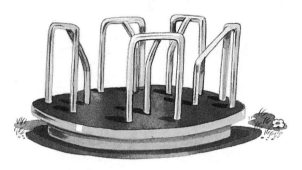

Chapter 11

Katie could barely hear the kids chanting anymore. The sound was muffled and distant. And she couldn't feel the warm sun on her back. Where was she?

There was only one way to find out where the magic wind had taken her. Slowly, Katie opened her eyes and looked around.

Wow! Somehow she'd landed in someone's office. A big office. Almost as big as her living room.

At the moment, Katie was standing behind a huge, dark wood desk. There were piles and piles of papers and folders stacked all over it. Whoever she'd turned into sure had a lot of work to do.

There were two big flags standing in the corner of the office. One was the red, white, and blue American flag. The other was a white flag with two red cherries on it. Katie had seen it before, in her school auditorium. That was the Cherrydale flag.

Which meant she was still in Cherrydale. What a relief! The magic wind hadn't blown her very far.

So now Katie knew where she was. Well, sort of, anyway. But she still didn't know *who* she was.

Katie looked down at her feet. Her way-cool orange and green sneakers were gone. She was wearing big, brown men's shoes instead.

Katie had been switcherooed into a man. A man with huge feet!

And hairy knuckles! *Yuck!*

Now Katie knew she'd turned into a

big-footed, hairy man. But *which* big-footed, hairy man?

She looked around the office for a clue. There were pictures on the walls.

Mayor Fogelhymer with Olympic skater Kerry Gaffigan.

Mayor Fogelhymer with Katie's favorite author, Nellie Farrow.

Mayor Fogelhymer with the Cherrydale High School football team.

Mayor Fogelhymer in ugly orange and yellow swim trunks on a beach with his family somewhere.

Katie made a face. *If I were mayor, I'd get a nicer pair of swim trunks*, she thought.

And then it hit her. She was the mayor! The magic wind had switcherooed her into Mayor Fogelhymer.

Right before his big meeting with the garage builders.

This was sooooooo . . . good! Really good!

Katie smiled. She had never been happy about a switcheroo before. Ever. But this time it was great. She was the mayor, and at the meeting, she would be able to tell everyone that she'd changed her mind about the parking lot. There would be a new playground instead.

Katie would be a hero!

Just then, the office door opened. A woman with gray hair poked her head inside. "Mr. Mayor?" she said.

"Yes. That's me!" Katie exclaimed happily.

The woman looked at her curiously. "I know who you are," she said. "I've been your assistant for four years."

Katie blushed. "Oh."

"I just wanted to let you know that the men from the Gray Metal Parking Garage Company are here," the woman explained. "Are you ready to meet with them?"

"Oh, yes!" Katie replied. "Bring 'em on!"

The meeting didn't last long. Ten minutes later, Katie walked out onto the steps of City Hall.

"I have a big announcement for you kids!" she shouted in her best mayor-sounding tone.

The kids all stopped chanting. They stood very still and looked up at Katie.

The news reporters rushed to the steps of City Hall. Some focused their cameras in Katie's direction. Others shoved microphones in her face.

Katie gulped. It was kind of scary having everyone stare at her like that. But that was what people did when the mayor spoke. And Katie was the mayor now.

So she spoke. "After a lot of thought and a really short meeting, I have made my decision about the empty lot next to the Cherrydale Arena. We are going to build a playground! A really great playground. Huge. With more than just swings, slides, and monkey bars. We're

going to have a rock-climbing wall, a sandbox for little kids, a sprinkler for when it gets really hot, and a vomit wheel." She stopped for a minute. Vomit wheel didn't sound very mayor-like. "I mean, one of those merry-go-round things kids spin on," she said quickly.

Nobody in the crowd said anything for a second. And then, suddenly, the kids began to cheer.

"Yeah, Mayor Fogelhymer!"

"The mayor rocks!"

"We're gonna get a playground!"

"Oh, yeah!"

Katie smiled really wide. She had never made so many people happy at one time. It felt terrific!

"I love being mayor!" she shouted out into the crowd.

Chapter 12

Katie was feeling extra good about herself as she walked back into City Hall. As soon as she reached his big corner office, she sat down behind Mayor Fogelhymer's desk and leaned back in his chair.

The mayor's assistant peeked her head in the door once again. This time, though, she had a very worried look on her face.

"Can I get you something, Mr. Mayor?" she asked Katie. "Maybe a coffee and some aspirin?"

"Coffee?" Katie made a face. "*Blech!* I hate coffee. And why would I need aspirin?

I don't have a fever."

Now the assistant looked more worried than ever. "I just thought that after a tough decision like that . . ."

"There wasn't anything tough about it," Katie said. "Those kids out there wanted a playground. I gave them what they wanted. Isn't that what mayors do?"

"Well . . ." the assistant began slowly. "You're the mayor. I'm sure you know what you're doing."

"Exactly!" Katie exclaimed, trying really hard to sound like a grown-up. "And right now I'm celebrating. Can I please have an orange soda?"

"An orange soda," the assistant repeated. She shook her head slightly. "Coming right up, sir."

Katie was so happy. Finally, this time, when the magic wind came and turned her back into Katie Kazoo, she wouldn't be leaving a big mess behind. In fact, this time, she had done the mayor a huge favor. Maybe she'd even get a medal or something.

Rrringg! Just then, the mayor's telephone rang. Katie wasn't sure what she should do. Did mayors answer their own telephones? Didn't their assistants do that?

But since Mayor Fogelhymer's assistant was busy getting Katie a soda, Katie decided to answer the phone herself.

"Hi," she said as she picked up the receiver.

"Is this Mayor Fogelhymer?" a woman on the other end asked.

"Yes," Katie replied.

"My name is Mary Sue Vining, and I wanted to speak to you about your decision to build a playground in that empty lot," the woman told Katie. "I just saw you on TV."

"Oh, you don't have to thank me," Katie said. "It was my pleasure."

"Don't worry," Mrs. Vining replied. "I'm not calling to thank you."

"You're not?" Katie asked.

"No. I'm really angry," Mrs. Vining told her. "I'm the president of the Cherrydale Garden Club. I called your office a week ago and asked if we could have a flower garden in that lot. One of your staff members told me that was impossible. She said that the only thing going in that empty lot was a parking garage."

Katie was surprised and kind of scared. Mary Sue Vining sounded very angry. "Well, um, I changed my mind," Katie told her. "Isn't a playground better than a parking garage?"

"I don't care if it's a playground or a garage," Mary Sue Vining said firmly. "If it's not a garden, I'm unhappy. I wanted to plant something beautiful in the empty lot. Something everyone—not just kids—could enjoy."

"Oh," Katie said quietly. "I'm really sorry you feel that way."

"I was angry enough when you said you were putting in a parking lot. But I was still going to vote for you," Mrs. Vining told Katie. "Now I know you lied to me. I could never vote for a liar! And I'm going to make sure none of the other members of the Garden Club vote for you, either!" She slammed down the phone.

Katie sat there for a minute. That had been kind of scary. She hoped the mayor wouldn't be too upset about losing the votes of the gardeners.

Still, there couldn't be that many of them. There were far more kids than Garden Club members.

Then Katie remembered something. Kids couldn't vote.

Rrringg! Just then, the phone rang again.

Katie was afraid to answer it.

Rrringg! Rrringg!

Whoever was on the other end wasn't hanging up. Katie would have to pick up the phone.

"Hello?" she said quietly.

"Mayor Fogelhymer, this is Colleen Barker," the woman on the other end of the phone said.

Katie smiled brightly. She knew Mrs. Barker very well. She was the director of the Cherrydale Animal Shelter. That was where Katie had found her dog, Pepper, when he was just a puppy.

"Hello, Mrs. Barker," Katie said. "I'm so happy to talk to you."

"Well, I'm *not* happy to talk to you!" Mrs. Barker exclaimed. "I asked you a few days ago about turning that empty lot into a dog run for our shelter dogs. You told me you'd already decided on a parking lot. You said we needed more parking around the arena."

"I sort of changed my mind," Katie explained. "Don't you think kids need a place to play?"

"So do dogs," Mrs. Barker said firmly. "What are you? Some sort of animal hater?"

Katie gasped. No one had ever called her

that. Katie was an animal lover. The biggest. She didn't even eat meat.

"I love animals," Katie insisted.

"Well, animal lovers *don't* love you!" Mrs. Barker told her. "And you'll find that out on Election Day."

As she hung up the phone, Katie blinked, hard. She didn't want to cry. She had a feeling there wasn't any crying allowed in politics.

And she'd already caused Mayor Fogelhymer enough trouble.

Rrringg!

Oh, no. There was the telephone again.

Rrringg!

But this time, the phone stopped after just two rings.

Good. Katie just wanted to sit there quietly in the office. Alone.

A moment later, the mayor's assistant poked her head into the office again. "Mr. Mayor, it's Charlie Weaver on the phone. He's the head of

Cherrydale's traffic department. He wants to know where you think you're going to park all the cars that will be driving to the Cherrydale Arena now."

"I don't know!" Katie exclaimed. "I just wanted to help my friends."

"Your who?" the assistant asked.

Oops. "I mean, I wanted Cherrydale's children to have a great place to play," Katie said, trying to sound like a real mayor.

"Oh," the assistant said. "Well, what do you want me to tell Charlie Weaver?"

Katie jumped up from her chair. "Tell him I went to the bathroom!" she exclaimed.

Chapter 13

Katie raced down the hall at top speed to the restrooms. She stopped for a minute, thinking. She knew she was a fourth-grade girl. But to everyone else she looked like a grown-up man.

Should she go in the men's room? Or the women's room?

Katie couldn't bring herself to go into the men's room. It was just too weird. So she knocked on the women's room door.

"Hello? Anybody in there?" she asked.

Nobody answered. *Phew!*

Katie walked into the bathroom and went

over to the sink. She splashed some cold water on her face.

She looked up at the mirror. Mayor Fogelhymer's reflection looked back at her.

Katie started to cry. This whole thing had turned into such a mess! All she had wanted to do was make the kids of Cherrydale happy. She hadn't meant to upset everyone else in town.

But that's what she had done. Or at least that's what it felt like.

Just then, Katie felt a cool breeze blowing on the back of her neck. She looked around. There was only one window in the bathroom, and it was shut tight.

The breeze on the back of Katie's neck went from cool to cold.

Then it went from being a gentle breeze to a brisk wind.

A wind that was only blowing on Katie.

This was no ordinary wind. This was the magic wind!

The magic wind grew stronger and stronger then, whirling around Katie like a wild tornado. She grabbed onto the sink and held tight, just to keep from being blown away.

And then it stopped. Just like that.

Katie Carew was back!

And Mayor Fogelhymer was standing right beside her.

"What are you doing here?" he asked Katie.

"I . . . um . . . I had to go the bathroom," Katie lied. She couldn't exactly tell him the truth, could she?

"In the men's room?" Mayor Fogelhymer asked her.

"Actually, this is the women's room," Katie replied.

Mayor Fogelhymer's cheeks grew red. "Oh, dear. Is anyone else in here?"

"Just you and me," Katie assured him. "And I'm leaving now."

"Me too," the mayor said. He hurried out of

the women's room.

In the hallway, Katie asked, "Are you okay? You don't look so good."

The mayor frowned. "I'm so confused. Why would I go into the women's room?"

Katie didn't say anything.

"Don't I know you?" the mayor asked her.

"I'm Katie Carew. You spoke at my school the other day."

"Oh, of course," Mayor Fogelhymer said. "Nice to see you again. But I have to go back to my office. I have a lot of work to do."

Katie frowned. "I wouldn't go back there right now."

"Why not?" the mayor wondered.

"Well, the phone is ringing and ringing," Katie said.

The mayor looked at her curiously. "How do you know that?"

"Um . . . well . . . I heard it when I walked past your office," she answered quickly. There.

That sounded believable.

"Oh. Well, that's okay. My phone always rings a lot. Especially around election time," the mayor told Katie. "It's probably some of my supporters."

Katie shook her head. "I don't think so," she said. "I think it's people who are mad that you decided to build a playground in the empty lot."

"I decided *what?*" Mayor Fogelhymer exclaimed. Then he stopped. "Wait, I think I remember . . . Did I really announce that in front of all the kids and the news cameras?"

Katie nodded slowly.

"Oh, no," Mayor Fogelhymer groaned. "That wasn't what I wanted to do at all. Cherrydale needs parking! And I promised. Oh, dear. I could lose the election over this!"

Katie looked sadly at the floor. It was all her fault.

When Katie got home Saturday afternoon,

she went right to the computer and tried to work on her report about President Truman. But she just couldn't stay focused on her work. There was too much else to think about.

Like the election speech she would have to give on Monday. Katie had no idea what she could promise the kids in school that would make them want to vote for her. She had a feeling that no matter what she promised to do, someone in the grade would want something else. Sooner or later, her friends would be mad at her—at least some of them.

That was pretty much what was happening to Mayor Fogelhymer. Thanks to Katie's big announcement about the playground, he could lose the election—and his job.

Katie sighed heavily and looked back at the computer. There was so much information about President Truman. He had a very long life. She didn't know what to work on first.

George and Kadeem were so lucky. Because

they had compromised, each of them only had to do half of President Kennedy's life.

Katie's eyes burst wide open. A big smile formed on her face.

"That's it!" she exclaimed.

Quickly, Katie opened the desk drawer and pulled out a clean sheet of paper and some colored pencils.

Once again, Katie Kazoo had gotten a great idea!

Chapter 14

As soon as her drawing was finished, Katie rode her bike over to City Hall. She hurried inside and ran down the long hall to the mayor's office.

A crowd of reporters and photographers was outside the mayor's office. They were making the mayor's assistant crazy.

"What's going on?" Katie asked one photographer.

"We're waiting for the mayor to come out and talk to us," the photographer told her. "He's in big trouble with the voters because of that playground. It's a major news story!"

Katie frowned. She sure hoped she could fix things for Mayor Fogelhymer.

Just at that moment, the mayor opened his office door. The reporters shoved microphones in his face. The photographers began snapping pictures.

"Mr. Mayor, do you have any comment?" one reporter asked.

"How do you explain your decision to build a playground?" another reporter shouted.

Mayor Fogelhymer's eyes darted from one person to another. Katie thought he might be looking for a friendly face. So she began waving her arms back and forth. "Yoo-hoo!" she shouted. "Mayor Fogelhymer!"

The mayor looked at her. He smiled with relief. "Hi, Katie!" he exclaimed.

Katie was proud. The mayor of Cherrydale actually remembered her name.

"I have to talk to you about something," Katie told him. "It's really important."

Mayor Fogelhymer nodded. "Of course, Katie," he said in a really loud voice. "I will meet with you. My office is always open to the people of Cherrydale."

Mayor Fogelhymer wrapped his arm around Katie's shoulders and smiled for the cameras. He was acting like he was her best friend.

At least until they got into his office. Once the news reporters were no longer there, Mayor Fogelhymer was less friendly.

"What is it?" he asked Katie. "I'm kind of busy today."

"It's about the playground," Katie began.

"Oh, that," the mayor interrupted. "I don't want to hear another word about it. That empty lot has caused me enough trouble as it is."

"But I have an idea," Katie insisted. "A great one. It will make so many people happy. All different kinds of people. You could get more votes with this plan." She held up her drawing. "See? It's a compromise."

"Votes?" the mayor repeated. He sounded interested.

Katie nodded. "Oh, yes. With my plan, you'll make the gardeners, the animal lovers, the drivers, *and* the kids happy."

The mayor sighed. "What have I got to lose?" he muttered as he sat down behind his desk. "Show me what you have."

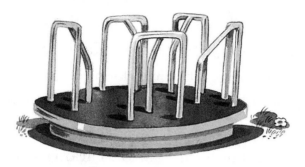

Chapter 15

Katie smiled brightly as she read the headline in the newspaper on Sunday morning.

"I don't know why I didn't think of this before," the mayor said in the newspaper article. "Luckily, I had a very smart adviser."

Of course, the mayor didn't mention that his adviser had been a ten-year-old girl!

There was a photograph of Katie's carefully drawn map next to the article in the newspaper. It showed the empty lot with a space for a new playground, a place for a dog run, and a fenced rose garden bordering the lot. Parking spaces for cars were put all around the outside of the park.

"I tried to address the needs of all the citizens of Cherrydale," the mayor said in the article. "That has always been my goal as mayor."

Katie tried to keep that in mind when she went upstairs to write her speech. Tomorrow she would have to tell all the kids in the fourth grade why they should vote for her. That wasn't going to be easy.

Katie wondered if Suzanne was having trouble with her speech. *Probably not.* Suzanne never had any problem telling people how great she was. She did it all the time.

But Katie wasn't like that. She didn't like to brag.

Still, she was going to have to brag if she was going to have a chance to become the mayor of the fourth grade. So Katie decided to make a list of all the best things about herself.

- I am a good artist
- I know how to make really yummy tomato sauce
- I am kind to animals
- I am brave enough to ride on rollercoasters that flip upside down
- I have a lot of friends
- I try to be nice

Katie sat there for a minute and stared at the piece of paper in front of her. Those were all really good things. They just weren't very mayor-ish.

Still, having a lot of friends was important. After all, your friends would probably vote for you in an election.

Unfortunately, Suzanne and Andy also had a lot of friends in the fourth grade. In fact, all three of them shared a lot of the same friends. Which meant Katie couldn't really count on anyone's vote in tomorrow's election.

Except her own, of course!

Chapter 16

Katie was feeling a little better about her speech by the time she arrived at school on Monday morning. Emma W. had helped her with it. Katie was going to say how important it was for a mayor to be nice. After all, a mayor had to get along with everyone, not just her best friends.

"I told you there would be a playground in that empty lot," Katie heard Suzanne boasting to Mandy in the schoolyard.

Oh, no! Was Suzanne still arguing about that?

"Yeah, well, there's going to be lots more

parking there, too," Mandy said.

"Maybe," Suzanne agreed. She smiled at all the kids standing around. "But I promised there would be a playground. And I got you all a playground."

"You didn't get it for us," Jeremy insisted. "We were all at the protest."

"Not all of us," Suzanne told him. She pointed at Katie. "She wasn't there."

All the kids stared at Katie.

Katie didn't know what to say. It wasn't like she could tell them what had actually happened to her at City Hall.

So instead, she just said, "I was there, Suzanne. I just had to go to the bathroom."

There. That was the truth. Sort of. After all, she *had* wound up in the bathroom.

"You must have had to go real bad," Suzanne said in a mean voice. "Because you were gone a long time."

Katie didn't answer.

Suzanne smiled at the crowd of kids. "Vote for me," she told them. "Whatever you want, I promise to get it for you."

"That's impossible, Suzanne," Katie told her. "You can't make everybody happy all of the time."

"Of course I can," she insisted.

"No, you can't," Katie said.

Suzanne rolled her eyes. "Oh, Katie, you don't know a thing about being mayor."

"Oh yeah?" Katie almost said. But she stopped herself. She couldn't tell Suzanne that she had been mayor for at least an hour.

Luckily, Jeremy defended Katie. "Neither do you, Suzanne," he pointed out.

Suzanne rolled her eyes. "The mayor is the boss," she told Jeremy. "And I know how to be the boss of things."

Katie sighed. There was definitely no arguing with that.

A little while later, Katie joined the rest
of the fourth grade in the auditorium. It was
time for the candidates to give their speeches.
Suzanne, Katie, and Andy all sat on the stage
next to Mr. G. and Ms. Sweet.

"I'll go first." Suzanne jumped up and turned
to the kids. "A leader shouldn't be afraid to go
first," she boasted.

"Okay, Suzanne," Ms. Sweet said. "You can
go first. Andy, you'll go second, and Katie,
you'll be last."

"That's fine," Katie said.

"Okay," Andy agreed.

Katie looked over at Suzanne and Andy.
Andy was wearing a jacket and a tie. He looked
very grown-up.

Suzanne had changed into a red skirt and a
white shirt. The shirt had the words VOTE FOR
SUZANNE embroidered on it in glittery thread.
On her wrists, she was wearing red and white

shimmery bracelets.

Then Katie looked down at her own black and white checked shirt and black pants. She wished she had worn something more special.

But wait! She had brought something special to school.

Unfortunately, it was in her book bag— which was back in class 4A.

"Mr. G.?" Katie asked her teacher. "I left my new campaign poster in the classroom. I want to have it when I give my speech. Can I go get it?"

"Sure, Katie Kazoo, you *may* run back to the room for your poster," Mr. G. said. "But hurry. I'm sure you want to hear what Suzanne and Andy have to say."

"I promise to be quick!" Katie agreed. She ran out of the auditorium at top speed.

Class 4A was completely quiet when Katie got there. The only one in the room was Slinky, the class snake. He didn't make any noise at all.

Katie found her backpack and her poster. Suddenly, she felt a cool breeze blowing on the back of her neck.

She looked over to see if a window was open.

Nope. They were all shut tight.

But there was definitely a breeze in the room. And it was getting colder and stronger.

It was also blowing only on Katie.

"Oh, no!" she shouted out. "Go away, magic wind! I have a speech to make!"

But the magic wind did *what* it wanted *when* it wanted. And right now, it wanted to spin around Katie.

The wind was blowing hard and cold now. It was spinning wildly, like a tornado. Katie shut her eyes and tried not to cry as the magic wind kept whirring around and around.

And then it stopped. Just like that.

One, two, switcheroo.

Good-bye, Katie Kazoo.

Hello . . . *who*?

Chapter 17

Katie could hear the sound of kids whispering and giggling. Slowly, she opened her eyes.

She was on the stage in the auditorium. A lot of kids were facing her. They weren't just any kids, either. They were the Cherrydale Elementary School fourth-graders.

What a relief. That wind had been so strong, she wasn't sure where she would wind up. But she was right where she belonged. Maybe this time, the magic wind hadn't switcherooed her at all.

She looked down at her shoes. Uh-oh. Her

black loafers were gone. Instead, she had on white shoes with little heels.

Her black pants were gone, too. Now she was wearing a red skirt and a white shirt.

A white shirt that said VOTE FOR SUZANNE in glittery thread!

Uh-oh!

No. This is impossible, Katie thought. *The magic wind already switcherooed me into Suzanne—that time during the modeling show. It's never turned me into the same person twice.*

At least not until now.

Katie reached up and touched her head. Instead of her loose red curls, Katie felt Suzanne's tight braids on either side of her face.

Katie gulped. She was Suzanne, all right.

This was sooooooo not good.

Now Katie was going to have to go up there and give a speech about why Suzanne should be elected mayor of the fourth grade.

For a second, Katie thought about telling everyone to vote for Katie instead of Suzanne. Or maybe making up a speech about how Katie would be a better mayor.

That would be pretty amazing—since the kids would think it was Suzanne doing the talking! Katie would probably get lots and lots of votes.

But that would be really unfair. And besides, Katie wanted to be elected because she was the best candidate. Being the best candidate meant being an honest and fair kid. It meant being nice.

An honest, fair, and nice kid wouldn't pull a trick like that!

Katie sighed. She was going to have to give a speech like the one she thought Suzanne would give—if she were here right now. No matter how mad she was at Suzanne, Katie knew that was the right thing to do.

But she didn't know Suzanne's speech. She

only knew her own.

Katie frowned. This was sooooooo not good.

Ms. Sweet walked over to the microphone.

"Boys and girls, let's quiet down now," she said.

There was a little more whispering and giggling, and then the auditorium became quiet.

"Great," Ms. Sweet complimented the kids. "You all know what an important day this is. I want everyone to listen carefully to what your candidates have to say. That will help you decide who you want to vote for. Our first candidate is Suzanne Lock."

Chapter 18

Ms. Sweet moved out of the way so
Suzanne could speak into the microphone.

But nothing happened. Everyone just sat
there.

"Suzanne?" Ms. Sweet asked. She looked
right at Katie.

"Oh, right," Katie said quickly. "Suzanne.
That's me."

The kids all began to giggle. Katie could
feel her cheeks burning as she walked up to
the podium.

She stared out at the kids.

The kids stared back.

Katie knew she had to say something. So she said the most Suzanne thing she could think of.

"Hi," she said. "I'm Suzanne Lock. I'm running for mayor of the fourth grade. You should vote for me because when I become famous—*and I will be*—our school will become famous, too, because of me."

A few of the kids in the audience groaned. Katie didn't blame them. That was a kind of silly thing to say. She had to come up with something better. Quickly, she tried to think of some of the things Suzanne had said during the campaign.

The stuff that wasn't mean about *her*, anyway.

"I . . . um . . . I think I would be a good mayor because the mayor is the boss of the grade," Katie said, trying to remember Suzanne's exact words. "And I'm . . . um . . . really bossy."

"You sure are!" George shouted back.

Katie blushed. No. That wasn't what she'd

meant to say. Not at all. "I mean, I'm good at taking charge of stuff," she corrected herself. "And I dress really nicely. And I would look good at a ribbon cutting."

A lot of kids began to laugh now.

"What are you talking about?" Kevin called up to her.

"You know, like when they open a new bridge," Katie said. "The mayor cuts the ribbon."

"Where would we put a bridge in school?" Kadeem asked.

The kids laughed harder.

Uh-oh. Katie gulped. Nothing was coming out right. And the more the kids laughed, the more confused Katie got.

What made it worse was the kids thought it was *Suzanne* who was all mixed up. And no matter how mad Katie was at Suzanne, she would never want to make her look like a fool in front of the whole fourth grade. Not on purpose, anyway. She had to do something to stop this.

What would Suzanne do? Katie thought.

She would probably smile and make it all seem like a big joke.

So that's what Katie did. She opened her mouth and tried to give a huge Suzanne smile.

But Katie *wasn't* Suzanne. And she didn't know how to smile like Suzanne. Katie's fake smile made her look like one of those happy face symbols on the computer.

"Suzanne, are you okay?" Ms. Sweet asked. "You look kind of ill."

Katie did feel sick. And embarrassed. She didn't know what to do. She just wanted this to be over.

So she ran off the stage and hurried into the hall.

Luckily, there was no one in the hall. Katie plopped down on the cold, hard floor and curled her knees up to her chest. Then she started to cry.

Suddenly, Katie felt a cool breeze blowing on the back of her neck. She looked around. All of the windows were shut. And there was no air-conditioning blowing overhead. This was November, after all. It was too cold outside for air-conditioning.

Speaking of cold, that wind was getting really chilly now. And powerful, too. In fact, it was blowing really, really hard.

This was no ordinary wind. This was the magic wind!

The magic wind began to spin, whirring all around Katie like a giant tornado. It was so powerful, Katie was pretty sure it was going to blow her someplace far, far away. She clutched her knees and shut her eyes tight.

And then it stopped. Just like that.

Katie Kazoo was back.

So was Suzanne. And boy, was she confused.

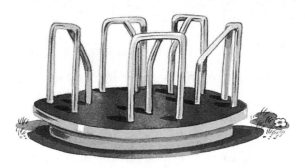

Chapter 19

"Katie, what are you doing out here?" Suzanne asked. She looked around the hallway. "What am *I* doing out here?"

"Well . . . um . . ." Katie stammered. She wasn't sure what to say.

"Never mind," Suzanne said. "I have to get back in there. I have a speech to make." She stopped for a minute. "Don't I?" she asked.

Katie shook her head. "You already made your speech," she said.

Suzanne looked curiously at Katie. "I made my speech?"

Katie nodded. "Yes."

"Oh, man." Suzanne slapped her forehead. "You mean I really said all that weird stuff about bridges and ribbon cutting?"

Katie nodded again.

"I don't understand why I would get all weird up there," Suzanne groaned. "It was like I was two different people or something."

Katie sighed. That was *exactly* what it was like.

But Katie didn't say that. Instead, she told Suzanne, "You've kind of been like a different person this whole campaign. You've been really awful."

"I just want to win," Suzanne explained. "Don't *you* want to win?"

Katie thought about that. She remembered how she'd felt when she had first switcherooed into Suzanne. She'd thought about making a speech telling everyone to vote for Katie. But she didn't.

"I want to win," Katie told Suzanne quietly.

"But not if it means hurting you or Andy."

Suzanne looked at the floor. "Oh."

The girls sat there for a minute, not saying anything. Finally, Suzanne turned to Katie. "I'm probably not going to win now, anyway," she said quietly.

Katie shrugged. Suzanne looked really sad.

"If I can't win, I guess I hope you do," Suzanne continued.

Wow. Katie was kind of surprised to hear Suzanne say something that nice.

"Thanks," Katie said. The girls walked back to the auditorium together.

* * *

Andy's speech was just ending when Suzanne and Katie arrived back at the auditorium. Katie could hear the kids applauding loudly.

"It must have been a good speech," Katie whispered to Suzanne as the girls climbed back up onto the stage.

Suzanne shrugged.

Ms. Sweet turned to Katie and Suzanne. "Oh, good, the girls are back," she said. "Katie, we're ready to hear from you."

Katie nodded. "Hi, there. I'm Katie Carew," she began. "I want you to vote for me because I am your friend. Friends always try to help each other. And if I am your mayor, that's what I promise to do for you."

Chapter 20

After lunch, Katie and Suzanne walked out into the yard together. They were both really nervous. The fourth-graders had voted right after the speeches. But Mr. G. and Ms. Sweet weren't going to announce the winner until after recess.

Katie had voted for herself. She also knew Suzanne had voted for *her*self. But what about everyone else? Who had the other fourth-graders voted for?

"I can't believe no one will tell me," Suzanne complained.

"Mr. G. said our votes were supposed to be

kept secret," Katie explained. "Just like in real elections."

"I know, but it's driving me crazy," Suzanne said. "I think you won."

Katie shook her head. "No way. You won. People think of you as a leader."

"But they really like you," Suzanne insisted.

"They like you, too," Katie replied.

"But you . . ." Suzanne began. Then suddenly, the two girls began to giggle.

"I can't believe we're arguing about *this* now," Katie said.

They both laughed.

A few minutes later, the bell rang. Recess was over.

It was time to find out who the new fourth-grade mayor was.

Suddenly, Katie felt butterflies fluttering all around in her belly. No, not butterflies. This was much worse. Katie was so nervous, it felt as though she had kangaroos hopping up and down in her belly.

Once again, the fourth grade piled into the school auditorium. Katie, Andy, and Suzanne all sat in the front row now.

Nobody said a word as Mr. G. climbed the stairs and went up on the stage.

"I want to say congratulations to all our candidates," Mr. G. said. "It takes a lot of courage to run for public office. You are all winners in my book."

Katie smiled. She felt very proud of herself.

"But there can be only one fourth-grade mayor," Mr. G. continued. "And that person is . . . Andrew Epstein!"

Andy stood up, turned around, and took a bow.

The kids behind Katie began to cheer.

"Yeah, Andy!" Kevin cheered.

"Mayor Epstein!" Mandy howled.

"Woo-hoo!" Manny shouted.

Suzanne turned around in her seat.

"Manny!" she shouted. "Why are you cheering? I thought you were on my team."

Manny shook his head. "I said I would help you make posters and stuff," he told Suzanne. "I didn't say I would vote for you."

"Why did you vote for Andy?" Katie asked Manny curiously.

"He called me the other day and asked what I thought the school needed," Manny explained. "I said a computer club. And he said he would talk to Principal Kane about it."

"He called me, too," Mandy piped up. "I said we needed better gym equipment. Andy suggested some ways to raise money to buy more balls and jump ropes and stuff."

"Wow," Katie said.

"I didn't know Andy was calling people to see what was important to them," Suzanne said. "Is he allowed to do that?"

"Of course he is." Katie sighed. While she and Suzanne were busy fighting with each other, Andy was acting like a real candidate. "I guess the best person really did win."

Suzanne didn't answer. Instead, she walked over to where Andy and a few of the boys were standing.

"Where are you going?" Katie called after her.

"To talk to Andy," Suzanne replied. "I have some great ideas about how to make me . . . I mean, my *school* . . . I mean, *our* school more famous."

Katie giggled. Well, at least she'd gotten that part of Suzanne's speech right!

Katie followed Suzanne. She didn't want to tell Andy what he should do. She just wanted to congratulate him on winning the election.

But before Katie could walk two steps, she felt a cool breeze blowing on the back of her neck.

A chill went up her spine.

Oh, no! Not the magic wind! She didn't want to switcheroo here, in front of everyone!

"George, please close that door," Ms. Sweet called toward the back of the auditorium. "It's cold outside. Don't you feel that wind?"

Phew. It wasn't the magic wind. It was just a regular old November wind.

Katie was sooo happy. She was going to stay a regular fourth-grade girl.

At least for now.

Twenty-five Fun Facts about the Presidents!

Katie and Suzanne definitely have Election Day fever! Lately, they've been amazing the rest of the fourth grade with really cool facts they've found about U.S. presidents. Now they're sharing those facts with you, so you can amaze your friends, too!

1. George Washington is the only president to have been inaugurated in two cities— New York and Philadelphia.

2. John Adams was the first president to live in the White House.

3. Thomas Jefferson had a pet mockingbird that sometimes flew around the White House.

4. The first president to be photographed was John Quincy Adams.

5. President Andrew Jackson was the only president to kill a man in a duel.

6. William H. Harrison was only president for thirty-two days. He got pneumonia after staying outside in the cold for too long during his inauguration and died.

7. President Zachary Taylor let his horse graze on the White House lawn.

8. The White House didn't have a bathtub until President Franklin Pierce ordered one put into one of the bathrooms.

9. James Buchanan was the only president who never married.

10. At 6' 4", Abraham Lincoln was the tallest president so far.

11. President Andrew Johnson's parents were too poor to send him to school. That's why he didn't learn to read until he was almost seventeen!

12. President Ulysses S. Grant was given a ticket for speeding while driving a horse and buggy through the streets of Washington, D.C.

13. Rutherford B. Hayes was the first president to have a telephone installed in the White House. Alexander Graham Bell, the inventor of the telephone, personally taught him how to use it.

14. The teddy bear was named after President Teddy Roosevelt.

15. Woodrow Wilson wasn't only president of the United States. He was also president of Princeton University.

16. Warren G. Harding was the first president to give a speech on the radio.

17. President Franklin Roosevelt was related by blood or marriage to eleven former presidents.

18. President Harry Truman's middle name was the letter *S*. He was named for both of his grandfathers.

19. President Dwight Eisenhower liked golf so much, he made sure a putting green was on the White House lawn, so he could practice while he was in office.

20. President John F. Kennedy's daughter, Caroline, had her own pony. His name was Macaroni.

21. President Richard M. Nixon was the only president to resign from office.

22. Before he became president, Ronald Reagan was a sports announcer for the Chicago Cubs as well as a movie and TV actor.

23. President George H.W. Bush hated broccoli so much that he banned the vegetable from the *Air Force One* menu!

24. When President Bill Clinton was a boy, he visited the White House and got to shake hands with another president—John F. Kennedy.

25. President George W. Bush once was an owner of the Texas Rangers baseball team, and he has a collection of more than two hundred and fifty signed baseballs.

About the Author

Nancy Krulik is the author of more than 150 books for children and young adults, including three *New York Times* bestsellers. She lives in New York City with her husband, composer Daniel Burwasser, their children, Amanda and Ian, and Pepper, a chocolate and white spaniel mix. When she's not busy writing the *Katie Kazoo, Switcheroo* series, Nancy loves swimming, reading, and going to the movies.

* * *

About the Illustrators

John & Wendy have illustrated all of the *Katie Kazoo* books, but when they're not busy drawing Katie and her friends, they like to paint, take photographs, travel, and play music in their rock 'n' roll band. They live and work in Brooklyn, New York.